Love at First Write: Balancing Love and Creativity

Rajesh Giri

Published by Rajesh Giri, 2023.

LOVE AT FIRST WRITE: BALANCING LOVE AND CREATIVITY

First edition. March 2, 2023.

ISBN: 979-8215070338

Written by Rajesh Giri.

Table of Contents

Dedication

To my beloved,

This book is dedicated to you, for being the source of my inspiration, motivation, and love. Your unwavering support and encouragement have fueled my creative passion and brought this story to life.

I am grateful for every moment we've shared, every laugh we've had, and every challenge we've overcome together. Your love has taught me the power of perseverance, kindness, and joy. It is because of you that I am able to write these words and share them with the world.

As you read this book, I hope it brings a smile to your face and warms your heart, just as you have done for me countless times. Thank you for being my partner in love and life, and for always inspiring me to reach for the stars.

With all my love,
Rajesh Kumar Giri
The Practical Success Coach

Legal Disclaimer

Copyright@Rajesh Kumar Giri - 2023

The work of fiction is purely fictional and any resemblance to actual persons, living or dead is coincidental. The characters, events, and dialogues portrayed in this book are products of the author's imagination and are not to be construed as real.

The author and publisher have made every effort to ensure that the information contained in this book is accurate and up-to-date at the time of publication. However, they assume no responsibility for errors, omissions, or damages that may arise from the use of the information contained herein.

This book is intended for entertainment purposes only and should not be used as a substitute for professional advice or treatment. The author and publisher do not assume any responsibility or liability for any actions taken by readers based on the information provided in this book.

Thank you for reading " **Love at First Write: Balancing Love and Creativity**".

Preface

Dear Reader,

I am delighted to present to you " **Love at First Write: Balancing Love and Creativity**," a romantic short creation that tells the story of two writers who meet and fall in love at a writing retreat.

Love is a powerful force that can inspire us to create and pursue our passions.

Reshma and Badal's love story is a testament to this truth. Their creative pursuits brought them together, but it was their shared love that kept them together.

As you turn the pages of this novel, you will be transported to an idyllic writing retreat where Reshma and Badal's love story unfolds. You will laugh with them, cry with them, and root for them as they navigate the challenges of balancing their creative ambitions with their growing feelings for each other.

But "Love at First Write" is more than just a romantic tale. It is also a story about the creative process and the pursuit of our dreams. As you follow Reshma and Badal's journey, you will gain insights into the writing process and the world of creativity, making this novel an ideal read for aspiring writers.

At its core, "**Love at First Write: Balancing Love and Creativity**" is a celebration of love, creativity, and the endless possibilities that come with pursuing our passions. I hope that you will find joy and inspiration in this story and that it will remind you of the power of love and the beauty of the creative process.

With love and admiration for the written word,

Rajesh Kumar Giri
The Practical Success Coach

Love at First Write: Balancing Love and Creativity

"Love at First Write: Balancing Love and Creativity" is a romantic short story about two writers who meet and fall in love at a writing retreat. It is a story of creativity, passion, and the struggles that come with balancing professional ambitions and personal desires.

The main characters, Reshma and Badal, are both aspiring writers who attend the same retreat to work on their craft. They are immediately drawn to each other, but their growing feelings for each other threaten to derail their writing goals.

As they navigate the challenges of their relationship and the pressures of the retreat, they discover new depths to their creativity and learn to find inspiration in unexpected places.

"Love at First Write: Balancing Love and Creativity" is a story about the power of love to inspire and motivate us, even as it challenges us to face our fears and push ourselves to be our best selves.

Let us clear the fact with a relaxing romantic poem

Pen and paper, our tools of the trade,

In a writing retreat, our love was made,
With every word, our hearts did unite,
But balancing love and work was no simple plight.

IDEAS FLOWED FREELY, our passion grew,
But deadlines loomed, and tensions ensued,
With compromise and dedication, we found our way,
Balancing love and creativity day by day.

Chapter 1: The Arrival

Reshma took a deep breath and stepped off the bus, her heart pounding with excitement and nerves. She had been looking forward to this writing retreat for months, and now that she was finally here, she felt a mix of anticipation and apprehension. She looked around at the sprawling estate, with its ivy-covered walls and manicured gardens, and felt a sense of awe.

This was the kind of place she had only read about in novels, and now she was going to spend the next two weeks living and working here.

As she made her way to the main house, she saw a group of writers gathered on the front lawn, chatting and laughing. She recognized a few faces from the online forums she had been following in the lead-up to the retreat, but most of them were strangers. She felt a twinge of anxiety as she approached the group, wondering if she would be able to fit in with these talented and experienced writers.

One of the writers, a tall man with sandy blond hair, caught her eye and smiled warmly. "Hi there," he said, extending a hand. "I'm Badal. You must be one of the new arrivals."

Reshma felt her cheeks flush as she shook his hand. "Yeah, I'm Reshma," she said. "Nice to meet you."

Badal introduced her to a few of the other writers, and Reshma soon found herself chatting and laughing with them like they were old friends. As they made their way to the main house for the opening reception, she felt a sense of excitement and belonging that she hadn't felt in a long time.

This was why she had come to the retreat, she realized. Not just to improve her writing skills, but to connect with other writers who shared her passion and her struggles. As she took her seat at the long banquet table and listened to the opening remarks from the retreat organizers, she felt a sense of optimism and possibility that she knew would stay with her long after the retreat was over.

Let us enjoy the chapter with a relaxing romantic poem
A ship on the horizon, a glimmer of light,
A journey to new lands, the start of a new sight,
The sea roars and the wind blows, as the ship draws near,
A journey to an unknown place, free of fear.

THE PORT AWAITS, WITH open arms,
A place to start, free from all harm,
The excitement builds, as we step on shore,
A new adventure, a place to explore.

THE PEOPLE HERE, WITH smiles so bright,
A new language, a new sight,

The sun sets on this new world,
Our hearts filled with love unfurled.

NEW FRIENDS AND NEW dreams, we find,
A new chapter of life, a new kind,
The journey continues, the adventure unfolds,
The arrival of a new story, waiting to be told.

Chapter 2: First Impressions

Over the next few days, Reshma and Badal found themselves drawn to each other. They attended the same workshops, sat next to each other at meals, and often found themselves lingering in the same spots around the estate. They talked about everything from their favorite books to their writing struggles to their shared love of hiking and nature.

Reshma felt a growing sense of connection with Badal, but she tried to push it aside. She had come to the retreat to focus on her writing, not to get distracted by a handsome stranger. Besides, she didn't want to be that person who fell for someone on the first day of the retreat. She had heard enough horror stories about writing retreat romances that ended in heartbreak and drama.

But as the days wore on, Reshma found herself thinking more and more about Badal. She noticed the way his eyes crinkled when he smiled, the way he always seemed to be able to find just the right words to say. She admired his dedication to his craft and his willingness to take risks with his writing.

One evening, as they sat together on the terrace overlooking the gardens, Badal turned to her and said, "You know, Reshma, I feel like we have a real connection. Something special."

Reshma's heart skipped a beat. She felt the same way, but she was afraid to admit it. "Yeah, I feel it too," she said, trying to keep her voice casual.

Badal leaned in closer. "I don't want to rush things, but I was wondering if you'd like to go for a walk with me tomorrow morning. Just the two of us. Maybe we could explore some of the trails around here."

Reshma hesitated for a moment, and then nodded. "That sounds nice. I'd like that."

As they said goodnight and went their separate ways, Reshma felt a mix of excitement and nerves. Was she really ready for this?

To let herself fall for someone so quickly, and at a writing retreat of all places?

But as she lay in bed that night, listening to the soft sound of crickets outside her window, she couldn't deny the flutter of anticipation in her chest.

Let us enjoy the chapter with a relaxing romantic poem

The eyes meet, a spark ignites,

A feeling in the heart, oh so bright,

The first impression, a lasting one,

A journey of love, has just begun.

THE WORDS SPOKEN, SO sweet and kind,

A connection made, two souls entwined,

The laughter shared, a joyful sound,

A new love, waiting to be found.

THE HEART BEATS FAST, the mind in a daze,
 A feeling so strong, in so many ways,
 The first impression, a leap of faith,
 A love story, waiting to take place.

THE FUTURE UNFOLDS, with each passing day,
 A love that blossoms, in every way,
 The first impression, a memory to keep,
 A love so true, forever to reap.

Chapter 3: The First Workshop

The next morning, Reshma met Badal at the entrance to the main house. They set off down one of the paths that wound through the estate, chatting about their writing goals and their favorite authors. Reshma felt a sense of ease and comfort with Badal that she had rarely felt with anyone else.

As they walked, they came across a small clearing with a table and chairs set up for a writing workshop. A group of writers was already gathered around the table, notebooks and pens at the ready.

Reshma felt a pang of regret that she hadn't brought her own notebook with her. She had been so focused on spending time with Badal that she had forgotten about the writing workshops that were a key part of the retreat.

But as the workshop got underway, she found herself getting caught up in the energy and enthusiasm of the other writers. The facilitator, a seasoned author with a warm smile and a kind demeanor, led them through a series of writing exercises designed to spark their creativity and get them thinking outside the box.

Reshma found herself scribbling furiously in her notebook, ideas and images flooding her mind faster than she could capture them. She felt a sense of exhilaration that she hadn't felt in a long time, a sense of being part of something bigger than herself.

As the workshop came to a close, Badal turned to her and said, "That was amazing. I feel so inspired right now."

Reshma nodded, feeling the same way. "Me too. I had forgotten how much I love being part of a writing community.

Let us enjoy the chapter with a relaxing romantic poem

In a room full of writers, I sat alone,

Nervously tapping on my phone,

I wondered if I had what it takes,

To create stories with depth and stakes.

THE AIR WAS THICK WITH anticipation,

As we waited for the workshop's initiation,

Then in walked a writer, tall and bold,

A presence that couldn't be ignored or sold.

WITH WORDS OF WISDOM and encouragement,

She led us on a journey of enlightenment,

The first workshop, a lesson so clear,

Writing is not just a hobby, but a career.

THE PENS STARTED MOVING, the ideas flowed,
    A creative energy, with passion and mode,
    The first workshop, a turning point,
    A chance to pursue dreams, to anoint.

THE NIGHT WAS LONG, the pages filled,
    A feeling of accomplishment, thrilled,
    The first workshop, a beginning so bright,
    A future of writing, with all our might.

Chapter 4: Balancing Writing and Romance

As the days passed, Reshma and Badal continued to spend more and more time together. They went on hikes, attended workshops, and shared meals and drinks in the evenings. Reshma felt herself falling for Badal more and more, but she also felt a nagging sense of guilt.

She had come to the retreat to focus on her writing, but she couldn't deny the strong feelings she had for Badal. She found herself torn between her creative ambitions and her growing desire to be with him.

One afternoon, as they sat together in the shade of a tree, Reshma broached the subject. "Badal, I have to be honest with you. I'm feeling a little conflicted about this. I came here to work on my writing, but I find myself getting distracted by you."

Badal took her hand and gave it a squeeze. "I understand, Reshma. Believe me, I do. But I also think that sometimes, the best way to fuel our creativity is by opening ourselves up to new experiences and connections.

And who knows? Maybe this could be the inspiration we both need to take our writing to the next level."

Reshma felt a sense of relief and gratitude wash over her. She had been worried that Badal would think she was being frivolous or flighty, but he seemed to understand exactly what she was going through.

Over the next few days, Reshma and Badal worked to strike a balance between their writing and their budding romance. They made a pact to spend at least a few hours each day working on their individual projects, and then to come together for walks, meals, and other activities.

Reshma found that having Badal as a writing partner actually helped her to stay more focused and disciplined. She was inspired by his work ethic and his willingness to take creative risks, and she found that their conversations sparked new ideas and insights.

By the end of the retreat, Reshma and Badal had both made significant progress on their writing projects, and they had also deepened their connection to each other. They exchanged contact information and promised to keep in touch, even as they returned to their separate lives.

As Reshma boarded the train back home, she felt a sense of joy and optimism that she hadn't felt in a long time. She knew that there would be challenges ahead, but she also knew that she had found something special in Badal, and that they would support each other through the ups and downs of their writing and their relationship.

Let us enjoy the chapter with a relaxing romantic poem

Pen in hand, mind awhirl,

Ideas sparked, emotions swirl,

A writer's life, full of passion,

But love's arrival, a new attraction.

HEARTSTRINGS PULL, a lover's glance,

Fueled by words, the romance advances,

The struggle now, to find the time,
To write the words, and make love rhyme.

A DELICATE BALANCE, love and art,
One feeds the soul, the other the heart,
A tug of war, within the mind,
As two passions, now intertwined.

BUT WITH EACH WORD, and every kiss,
Comes a sense of balance, and bliss,
For love and writing, need not compete,
But complement, and make life complete.

Chapter 5: Back to Reality

Reshma stepped off the train and took a deep breath. She was back in the real world now, away from the idyllic writing retreat and the blissful bubble of creative energy that she and Badal had shared. As she made her way through the station and out into the bustling city streets, she felt a sense of disorientation and anxiety.

She had been so focused on her writing and her burgeoning romance with Badal that she had almost forgotten about the rest of her life. She had bills to pay, a job to go back to, and a host of other responsibilities and obligations that had been temporarily forgotten.

As she walked to her apartment, Reshma couldn't help but feel a sense of melancholy. She missed Badal already, and she longed to be back in the beautiful surroundings of the retreat. But she also knew that she had work to do, both in terms of her writing and her personal life.

Over the next few weeks, Reshma threw herself back into her routine. She went back to her job as a marketing assistant at a local publishing company, and she spent her evenings and weekends working on her novel. She exchanged occasional emails and texts with Badal, but they both knew that their relationship would need to take a backseat to their other priorities for a while.

Despite the challenges of readjusting to her old life, Reshma found that she was more focused and productive than ever before. The time she had spent at the retreat had taught her how to tap into her creativity and stay disciplined in her writing, even when distractions and obligations threatened to pull her away.

As she neared the end of her first draft, Reshma felt a sense of satisfaction and pride that she had never felt before. She knew that the novel was far from perfect, but she also knew that it was the product of months of hard work and dedication. And she knew that she had Badal to thank for much of her success.

With the first draft of her novel complete, Reshma decided to take a break from writing and focus on her personal life. She made plans with friends, went on dates, and tried to reconnect with the other parts of her identity that had been neglected during her time at the retreat.

But even as she moved forward with her life, Reshma couldn't help but think about Badal and the possibility of a future together. She knew that the road ahead would be long and uncertain, but she also knew that she was ready to take the leap and see where it would take her.

Let us enjoy the chapter with a relaxing romantic poem
We left the retreat with heavy hearts
Our love and passion in perfect parts
Now back to reality, our separate lives
The memory of our love, forever thrives

WE SAID OUR GOODBYES with a tearful embrace
A love like ours, hard to replace
But we knew deep down we'd meet again

And our love story would continue to begin

NOW IN OUR SEPARATE worlds, we continue to write
But thoughts of each other fill our minds each night
We balance our craft and our love with care
Knowing that our future, together we'll share

BACK TO REALITY, BUT our love still strong
We'll find our way back to where we belong
Until then, we'll keep our love alive
Writing our stories, waiting to thrive.

Chapter 6: A Surprise Visit

One day, Reshma was sitting at her desk at work when she received a text from Badal.

"I'm in town for the day," the message read. "Would you like to meet up?"

Reshma's heart skipped a beat as she read the message. She had been missing Badal so much, and the thought of seeing him again filled her with excitement and nerves.

She quickly replied, "Of course! Where should we meet?"

Badal suggested a coffee shop near Reshma's office, and they arranged to meet there in an hour.

As Reshma rushed to finish up her work, she couldn't help but wonder what it would be like to see Badal again. Would they pick up where they left off, or would things be awkward and strained?

When she arrived at the coffee shop, she saw Badal sitting at a table near the window. He looked up and smiled as she approached, and Reshma felt her nerves begin to ease.

They hugged briefly, and then sat down to catch up over coffee. Badal told her about his latest writing projects and the workshops he had been leading, while Reshma shared her progress on her novel and the challenges she had been facing in her personal life.

As they talked, Reshma realized how much she had missed Badal's company and his support. They laughed and joked like they had at the retreat, and Reshma felt a sense of warmth and comfort that she had been missing since she had returned to the real world.

As they finished their drinks and prepared to say goodbye, Badal surprised Reshma by pulling out a manuscript from his bag.

"I wanted to give you this," he said. "It's a book I wrote a few years ago. I think you'll like it."

Reshma felt a surge of gratitude and joy as she accepted the manuscript. She knew that Badal had always been supportive of her writing, but this gesture felt like a sign of something deeper and more significant.

As they said their goodbyes and went their separate ways, Reshma couldn't help but feel hopeful and optimistic about the future. She knew that there were still many obstacles and challenges ahead, but she also knew that she had Badal by her side, and that was enough to make her feel like anything was possible.

Let us enjoy the chapter with a relaxing romantic poem

A surprise visit, unexpected and sweet

Heart racing, anticipation in full heat

Warm embrace, lips meeting in a kiss

Moment frozen in time, pure bliss

Days spent together, love growing strong

Writing and romance, a perfect song

But reality calls, and they must part

Leaving a piece of their heart

Distance and time, a challenge to overcome

But their love will endure, and never succumb

For in their hearts, a flame burns bright
A love born from that surprise visit, a beautiful sight.

Chapter 7: A Creative Collaboration

Over the next few weeks, Reshma and Badal continued to stay in touch, chatting on the phone and texting each other daily. They talked about their writing projects and offered feedback and encouragement to each other.

One day, Reshma had an idea. "What if we collaborated on a project?" she suggested over the phone.

Badal was intrigued. "What do you have in mind?"

"Well, I was thinking about a story where two writers meet at a writing retreat and fall in love, but struggle to balance their creative ambitions with their growing feelings for each other," Reshma explained.

Badal laughed. "That sounds like our story."

Reshma smiled. "Exactly! I think it would be a fun project to work on together. We could draw on our own experiences and insights to create something really special."

Badal agreed to the idea, and they began brainstorming plot points and character details. They set up a shared folder on Google Drive and started sharing notes and ideas.

As they worked on the project, Reshma and Badal found that their creative collaboration was bringing them even closer together. They talked more openly about their hopes and fears, and shared more personal stories and experiences.

Reshma felt like she was getting to know Badal on a deeper level, and she found herself falling even more in love with him. She began to wonder if their collaboration could lead to something more, something beyond just a creative partnership.

But at the same time, she was also hesitant. She didn't want to risk losing Badal's friendship and support, especially since their writing projects had become such an important part of her life.

As the weeks passed, Reshma and Badal continued to work on their collaborative project, their shared passion for writing bringing them closer together with each passing day. But Reshma couldn't help but wonder if they were both feeling the same way, or if she was just imagining things.

LET US ENJOY THE CHAPTER with a relaxing romantic poem
Two pens in hand, two minds as one
Together they create, a story begun
Their words dance on the page
A beautiful collaboration, a creative stage

IN EACH OTHER'S PRESENCE, they thrive
Inspiration flows, as they strive

To craft a tale, with love and heart
A masterpiece in the making, a work of art

THEIR PASSION FUELS, their writing fire
    As they work together, to inspire
    A bond is formed, a connection deep
    Their writing journey, forever to keep

A CREATIVE COLLABORATION, like no other
    Their words intertwine, as they discover
    The magic of writing, as a team
    Their dreams and goals, now a gleam.

Chapter 8: A Complicated Confession

One night, Reshma and Badal were on the phone, discussing the latest plot developments in their collaborative project, when Reshma found herself blurting out her feelings.

"Badal, I have to tell you something," she said, her heart pounding in her chest. "I think I'm falling in love with you."

There was a long pause on the other end of the line, and Reshma felt her anxiety growing. Had she just ruined everything?

Finally, Badal spoke. "Reshma, I think I'm falling in love with you too."

Relief flooded through Reshma, and she felt tears spring to her eyes. They talked for hours, sharing their fears and their hopes, and exploring the possibilities of a romantic relationship.

But as the conversation drew to a close, Badal hesitated. "I just have one question," he said. "What happens to our collaboration if we start dating?"

Reshma felt a pang of fear in her chest. She hadn't thought about that, and she didn't want to lose the creative partnership they had worked so hard to build.

"I don't know," she said honestly. "But I don't want to lose what we have, either."

Badal was silent for a moment. "Maybe we could take a break from the collaboration, while we figure things out?" he suggested.

Reshma nodded slowly. It made sense, but she still felt a twinge of sadness at the thought of putting their project on hold.

Over the next few days, Reshma and Badal talked more about their feelings and the future of their collaboration. They decided to take a break from working together for a little while, to focus on their romantic relationship and see where it led.

Reshma was nervous, but also excited. She had never felt this way about anyone before, and she couldn't wait to see where their relationship would go. But at the same time, she couldn't help but worry about what might happen to their creative partnership if things didn't work out between them.

Let us enjoy the chapter with a relaxing romantic poem
In the midst of words and ink
Feelings of love begin to sink
Creative minds so intertwined
A bond that's hard to define

A SECRET HELD FOR FAR too long
A confession that feels so wrong
Love and art, a complex mix
One that often leaves hearts fixed

TO CONFESS AND RISK it all
Or keep silent and just stall
A choice that weighs so heavily
A decision that's made so carefully

BUT IN THE END, THE truth must out
Or it will linger, cause doubts
A complicated confession made
A new path for love to be laid.

Chapter 9: A New Beginning

As Reshma and Badal embarked on their romantic relationship, they found that their writing was still a strong part of their lives. They may have taken a break from collaborating on their project, but they still talked about writing and shared their work with each other.

In fact, Reshma found that being in a relationship with someone who understood her creative process was inspiring. She felt like she could open up more about her work, and Badal's feedback was always thoughtful and constructive.

But there were also challenges. Reshma and Badal both had busy lives, with demanding day jobs and other commitments. Finding time to write, let alone to work on a joint project, became increasingly difficult.

They tried setting aside a regular writing time, but that often got disrupted by work emergencies or social commitments. They tried working on the project separately and sharing their work later, but that felt disjointed and unsatisfying.

It wasn't until they stumbled on a new idea that things started to come together again. One evening, while they were out for a walk, Reshma and Badal started talking about their favorite childhood books.

"I loved The Chronicles of Narnia," Reshma said. "And The Secret Garden. And I always wished I could write something like that."

Badal smiled. "You can," he said. "We can. Why don't we try writing a children's book together?"

Reshma's heart leapt at the idea. It was a new challenge, and something they could work on in short bursts of time. They could brainstorm ideas over dinner, or jot down notes on their lunch break.

They threw themselves into the project with enthusiasm, and soon found that they were making progress in ways they hadn't before. They were building a new creative partnership, one that was infused with the joy of writing and the joy of being in love.

As they worked on the book, they found that it was a perfect blend of their two styles. Reshma's love of whimsy and Badal's talent for plotting came together in a story that was both charming and suspenseful.

By the time they finished the book, Reshma and Badal had a new appreciation for the power of collaboration. They had found a way to make their creative partnership work, even as they navigated the ups and downs of their romantic relationship. And they were excited to see where their writing would take them next.

Let us enjoy the chapter with a relaxing romantic poem

The page has turned, a fresh start to begin,

The past left behind, new stories to spin,

A journey of love and creativity awaits,

The future unknown, but hope never abates.

A BLANK CANVAS, WAITING to be filled,

With words of passion, emotions distilled,
A new world to explore, a new story to tell,
With courage and conviction, we'll excel.

THE ROAD AHEAD MAY be winding and long,
But together we'll stand, and nothing go wrong,
With each other by our side, we'll take flight,
Into a world of endless possibilities, so bright.

A NEW CHAPTER OF OUR lives has begun,
And we'll write it together, till it's done,
With each word, a step closer to the end,
A new beginning, a new life to spend.

Chapter 10: The Next Chapter

With their children's book complete, Reshma and Badal felt a renewed sense of purpose and energy in their writing. They had proven to themselves that they could work together creatively, and they were eager to see what other projects they could tackle.

As they brainstormed ideas for their next project, they talked about the challenges they had faced in their personal lives over the past few months. Reshma's mother had been ill, and Badal had been dealing with a difficult coworker.

"I feel like there's a story in there," Badal said, tapping his pencil against his notebook.

Reshma looked at him quizzically. "What do you mean?"

"Well, think about it," Badal said. "We both had these struggles to overcome. Maybe we could write something about resilience, or perseverance. Something that would resonate with people who are going through tough times."

Reshma thought about it for a moment, and then nodded. "I like that idea," she said. "But I don't want it to be too heavy. Maybe we could write a romantic comedy, but with characters who are dealing with difficult situations."

Badal's face lit up. "Yes! That's perfect. We could have a couple who are going through some tough times, but who find each other and learn to support each other."

And so, they began work on their next project: a romantic comedy about two people who meet in the midst of personal struggles, and find solace and support in each other's company.

As they worked on the story, Reshma and Badal found that their own experiences gave them a deeper understanding of their characters' struggles. They wrote with empathy and compassion, creating characters who were flawed and real, but who also had the capacity for growth and change.

The more they worked on the story, the more they felt like they were onto something special. They could feel the magic of their partnership at work, as they bounced ideas off each other and refined their characters' arcs.

And as they wrote, they also deepened their own relationship. They had always been supportive of each other, but now they had a shared creative vision that made them feel even closer.

As they finished the first draft of the script, Reshma and Badal were already excited to start the revisions. They knew that this project would be a labor of love, one that would bring them even closer together.

Let us enjoy the chapter with a relaxing romantic poem

The pages turn, a new chapter begins,

A fresh start, as life constantly spins.

The story continues, the plot unwinds,

New characters emerge, with their own lines.

THE PAST IS GONE, BUT not forgotten,
Memories remain, some sweet, some rotten.
Lessons learned, mistakes to avoid,
New opportunities to be enjoyed.

THE FUTURE'S UNKNOWN, full of mystery,
But it's up to us to create our history.
With pen in hand, we write our fate,
And embrace the journey, whatever it may await.

Chapter 11: The Writing Retreat

With their script for the romantic comedy complete, Reshma and Badal decided to take a break from their usual routine and attend a writing retreat together.

The retreat was held at a secluded lodge in the mountains, surrounded by trees and wildlife. It was the perfect setting for writers to disconnect from the outside world and focus on their craft.

Reshma and Badal arrived on the first day, eager to immerse themselves in the retreat's workshops and writing sessions. They met other writers from all over the country, and soon found themselves forming new friendships and connections.

But as the days passed, Reshma and Badal found themselves drawn back to each other. They spent long hours working on their script, reading each other's work and offering feedback. They took walks in the woods, enjoying the quiet and the fresh air.

One night, as they sat outside by a campfire, Badal turned to Reshma and took her hand. "I know we're here to work on our writing," he said, "but I just have to say it. I'm so glad we're here together."

Reshma smiled, feeling the warmth of Badal's hand in hers. "Me too," she said. "This has been such an amazing experience, and it's made me realize how much I love working with you."

Badal leaned in and kissed her, and Reshma felt a rush of emotion. It was as if their whole relationship had been leading up to this moment, this perfect moment under the stars.

The rest of the retreat passed in a blur of writing sessions and socializing with the other writers. But Reshma and Badal knew that they had taken a major step forward in their relationship. They had found a new level of trust and intimacy, one that would carry them forward as they continued to work on their writing projects.

As they drove back home, Reshma and Badal talked excitedly about their plans for the future. They knew that they had something special, something that went beyond their individual writing talents. They had a true partnership, one that was grounded in love and creativity.

And as they drove, Reshma couldn't help but feel grateful for the chance encounter that had brought them together. It was love at first write, and it was a love that would only continue to grow stronger with each passing day.

LET US ENJOY THE CHAPTER with a relaxing romantic poem
A place of solace, a writer's dream,
A haven where creativity beams,
A tranquil space, far from the crowd,
Where words take flight, unbound.

THE RUSTLING LEAVES, the gentle breeze,
    The chirping birds, the buzzing bees,
    Inspiring thoughts, ideas galore,
    The mind races, wanting more.

THE BLANK PAGE, A CANVAS to fill,
    With characters, emotions, and skill,
    Pen to paper, fingers to keys,
    The magic flows, oh so sweetly.

THE WRITING RETREAT, a precious gem,
    A journey of self-discovery, a rare gem,
    A place to find oneself, anew,
    To write, create, and pursue.

Chapter 12: Balancing Love and Work

After the retreat, Reshma and Badal returned to their normal lives, but things were different now. They had grown closer and more connected during their time away, and they were eager to keep that momentum going.

But they quickly realized that it wasn't going to be easy. Both Reshma and Badal were ambitious writers, with deadlines and projects that demanded their attention. It was a constant struggle to balance their creative work with their growing relationship.

At first, they tried to keep their writing and their personal lives separate. They set aside certain times of the day for writing, and other times for spending time together. But that approach quickly proved to be too rigid and inflexible.

So they tried something else. They started collaborating on new projects, writing together and bouncing ideas off each other. They found that they were more productive when they worked together, and that they were able to inspire each other in new and unexpected ways.

But even that had its challenges. Sometimes they disagreed on creative decisions, and it was hard not to take those disagreements personally. And when they did have personal conflicts, it was hard not to let that spill over into their writing.

It was a delicate balancing act, but Reshma and Badal were determined to make it work. They loved each other deeply, and they knew that their partnership was worth the effort.

As the months went by, they learned to communicate better, to listen to each other's needs, and to find compromises when necessary. They learned to give each other space when needed, but also to lean on each other for support and encouragement.

And through it all, they continued to write, to create, and to grow together. They wrote a successful screenplay, and even started working on a novel together.

It wasn't always easy, but Reshma and Badal knew that they were doing something special. They were proving that it was possible to have both love and work, to balance passion with practicality.

And as they sat together at their desks, typing away on their keyboards, they couldn't help but smile at the knowledge that they had found something truly rare and wonderful. They had found love at first write, and they knew that they would keep writing their love story for years to come.

Let us enjoy the chapter with a relaxing romantic poem
In the hustle and bustle of life's daily grind,
It can be tough to balance love and work combined,
But when two hearts are determined to succeed,
There's nothing that can stop them, nothing impede.

THROUGH EARLY MORNINGS and long, late nights,
They strive to keep their love burning bright,
For love is a fire that can never be tamed,
And it's worth every sacrifice, every pain.

WITH EACH NEW CHALLENGE, they stand hand in hand,
Determined to weather every storm, every demand,
For they know that their love is the foundation,
That will see them through, no matter the situation.

AND SO THEY CONTINUE on this journey of life,
Balancing love and work, through joy and strife,
For they know that in the end, it will all be worth it,
For love is the sweetest reward, the ultimate profit.

Chapter 13: The Big Breakthrough

Reshma and Badal had been working on their novel for months, and they were feeling stuck. They had hit a wall in their creative process, and they couldn't seem to find a way to break through it.

They had tried everything – changing their writing location, taking breaks, even brainstorming with other writers – but nothing seemed to work. They were starting to worry that they would never finish their book.

But then, one night, Reshma had an idea. She woke up in the middle of the night with a fully-formed plot twist in her head, and she immediately grabbed her laptop and started typing.

She worked for hours, and by the time Badal woke up the next morning, she had written an entire chapter. Badal was amazed and inspired by her sudden burst of creativity, and he started writing as well.

For the next few days, they wrote furiously, feeding off each other's energy and enthusiasm. They finally found their groove, and they were amazed at how easily the words flowed.

Before they knew it, they had finished their book. They couldn't believe it – after months of struggling, they had finally broken through and found success.

They celebrated with a bottle of champagne, toasting to their hard work and perseverance. They knew that they had a lot of work left to do – editing, revising, and finding a publisher – but they were confident that they could handle it.

And they were right. Within a few months, they had found a literary agent who loved their book, and they soon had a publishing deal with a major publishing house.

Their book was a hit, and they were suddenly in demand as writers and speakers. They toured the country, doing book signings and speaking engagements, and they were amazed at the response they received.

They knew that they had each other to thank for their success. Without their love and partnership, they never would have been able to break through and find their creative voice.

As they sat together, basking in the glow of their newfound success, they couldn't help but feel grateful for each other and for the magic that they had found at that writing retreat so many months ago. They had proven that love and creativity could go hand in hand, and they were excited to see what the future held for them – both as writers and as partners.

Let us enjoy the chapter with a relaxing romantic poem
The words escape her, like birds in flight,
Her pen poised, she battles with might,
To capture the story in her head,
And bring her characters to life instead.

HER LOVE FOR WRITING consumes her days,
But balancing love is a tricky maze,

For she longs to spend time with her beau,
And let their love flourish and grow.

YET THE MUSE CALLS and she must write,
In the wee hours of the night,
But when her breakthrough finally comes,
She knows it's worth all the battles she's won.

HER PARTNER SUPPORTS her, day by day,
Encouraging her all the way,
Together they balance love and work,
And enjoy the fruits of their hard-earned perk.

FOR EVERY WORD ON THE page is a labor of love,
A product of their bond, sent from above,
And with each chapter, they grow and thrive,
Together, they embark on the next great drive.

Chapter 14: Balancing Love and Writing

Reshma and Badal had achieved their dream of becoming successful authors, but they soon realized that their newfound fame and busy schedules were putting a strain on their relationship.

They were constantly traveling and promoting their book, which left little time for each other. They were also working on their next book, which meant long hours spent writing and editing.

They knew that they needed to find a way to balance their writing careers and their relationship, but they weren't sure how to do it.

They started by setting aside time each day to spend together. They would go for walks, have dinner together, or just sit and talk. They also made a point of disconnecting from their phones and email during these times, so they could fully focus on each other.

They also made sure to schedule writing time separately, so they could each work on their individual projects without interruption. They found that this gave them the space they needed to be creative without feeling guilty about neglecting each other.

But perhaps the biggest breakthrough came when they started working on a joint project again. They realized that collaborating on a book was a way to bring them closer together and reignite their passion for writing.

They set aside time each week to work on their next book together, and they found that the process was even more enjoyable than the first time around. They had learned to trust each other's instincts and work together seamlessly.

They also found that writing together was a way to deepen their connection. As they wrote, they would discuss their ideas, their hopes, and their fears. They were able to share a part of themselves that they wouldn't have been able to otherwise.

As they finished their joint project, they both knew that they had found the perfect balance between their love and their writing careers. They had learned that with a little planning and a lot of communication, it was possible to have both.

And they were excited for what the future held – both as writers and as partners. They knew that they would face challenges along the way, but they were confident that they could handle anything as long as they had each other.

Let us enjoy the chapter with a relaxing romantic poem
Words swirl around my head,
Characters dance, plots unwind,
I scribble away, heart and pen in sync,
Passion and creativity entwined.

BUT THERE'S ANOTHER force in my life,
A love that tugs at my heart,
I try to balance both, to make time,
For writing and for love, not to fall apart.

SOMETIMES IT'S A STRUGGLE, a juggling act,
To find the right balance, to make it work,
But I know that both are worth the effort,
For love and writing, they both have their perks.

SO I TAKE A DEEP BREATH, focus my mind,
And pour my heart out on the page,
Balancing love and writing, with each line,
Building a life that's full of love and sage.

Chapter 15: Happily Ever After

Reshma and Badal's next book was a huge success, topping bestseller lists and receiving critical acclaim. But for them, the true success was the fact that they had found a way to balance their love and their writing careers.

They continued to collaborate on future projects, and their joint success only brought them closer together. They also continued to prioritize their relationship, making time for each other no matter how busy their schedules became.

As time went on, Reshma and Badal got engaged, and they decided to get married at the same writing retreat where they had first met. It was a beautiful and romantic ceremony, filled with the friends and colleagues who had been there for them throughout their writing journeys.

After their wedding, Reshma and Badal took some time off to travel and enjoy their new life as newlyweds. They visited exotic locations and enjoyed each other's company, taking in the beauty of the world around them.

As they traveled, they found that their experiences together only fueled their creativity. They wrote about the places they visited, the people they met, and the adventures they had. And through it all, they remained each other's biggest fans and supporters.

Years went by, and Reshma and Badal continued to write and publish successful books. They became known as the ultimate writing duo, and their fans eagerly anticipated each new release.

But for Reshma and Badal, the most important thing was their love and their partnership. They had proven that love and writing could coexist, and that the two could even complement each other.

And as they looked back on their journey, they knew that they had found their happily ever after – both in their personal lives and in their writing careers.

Let us enjoy the chapter with a relaxing romantic poem
In the end, they found their way,
Balancing love and work each day,
Through the highs and through the lows,
They learned to navigate the unknown.

THEIR LOVE GREW STRONGER with each page,
As they journeyed through life's stage,
Together they faced each new test,
And found joy in each other's quest.

THEIR WORDS FLOWED like a gentle stream,
And love was more than just a dream,
They found success beyond compare,
And knew that they were meant to share.

THEIR JOURNEY WAS LONG, but worth the ride,
As they discovered love's true guide,
And so they lived, hand in hand,
A love story that would never end.

Epilogue

Reshma and Badal continued to write together for the rest of their lives, but their success was never again as great as their first book. However, that didn't matter to them because they had each other and their love.

Years after they passed away, their first book was rediscovered and republished, and it quickly became a bestseller once again. It was then that the world truly recognized the incredible talent and love story that Reshma and Badal had shared.

Their love had been the inspiration for their writing, and their writing had been the expression of their love. They had truly lived a love story that would last forever.

Their legacy lived on through their writing and through the love they had shared. And for generations to come, they would continue to inspire writers and romantics alike, proving that love and creativity could coexist and flourish together.

Don't miss out!

Visit the website below and you can sign up to receive emails whenever Rajesh Giri publishes a new book. There's no charge and no obligation.

https://books2read.com/r/B-A-OWRS-WKEGC

BOOKS 2 READ

Connecting independent readers to independent writers.

Did you love *Love at First Write: Balancing Love and Creativity*? Then you should read *Beyond Time and Space: A Love That Endures*[1] by Rajesh Giri!

"Beyond Time and Space: A Love That Endures" is a heartwarming and emotionally captivating love story that spans across time and space.

This book tells the story of two people who are separated by time and distance, yet are brought together by an unbreakable bond that defies all odds.The book takes readers on a journey through different eras and locations, from medieval times to modern-day New York City, and explores the challenges that come with a love that transcends time and space.With vivid descriptions and engaging characters, this book is a true page-turner that will leave readers rooting for the protagonists and

---

1. https://books2read.com/u/4ENay0

2. https://books2read.com/u/4ENay0

their enduring love.This book also delves into the deeper themes of love, fate, and destiny, making it a perfect read for those who enjoy thought-provoking stories.Whether you're a fan of romance novels or simply love a good story that touches the heart, "Beyond Time and Space: A Love That Endures" is a must-read.

Beyond Time and Space: A Love That Endures is a comprehensive guidebook that delves into the secrets of sustaining a loving and lasting relationship. This book contains factual chapters, examples of real-life love stories, and relaxing romantic poetry to help readers understand the importance of love and connection in their lives.

Through engaging activities, the book guides readers on how to maintain love and connection with their partners, no matter the challenges they may face. From the importance of communication and trust to the role of empathy and compassion, this book covers all the essential facts needed to sustain a healthy and fulfilling relationship.

Furthermore, the book features example love letters that teach readers how to communicate effectively and build a strong foundation for their relationships. These letters demonstrate the power of words and how they can bring people together in a profound and meaningful way.

Whether you're in a long-term relationship or just starting out, Beyond Time and Space: A Love That Endures is a must-read book. It provides practical advice, insightful wisdom, and heartfelt inspiration that will help you nurture your relationship and keep the flame of love burning brightly. So, if you're ready to discover the secrets of a happy and enduring love story, this book is the perfect place to start.

Check the thrilling love letter before reading the whole book

My dearest Reshma,

As I sit down to write this letter, I am filled with longing for your presence. Even though miles separate us, our love is stronger than the distance that separates us.

"My love for you is as boundless as the ocean,

As timeless as the tides,

And as deep as the sea."

Every day, my heart aches to be near you, to feel your touch and to hear your voice. But until then, I will let my words carry my love across time and space to you.

I remember the day we met like it was yesterday. The way you smiled at me, the sound of your laughter, and the sparkle in your eyes - I knew I had found my soulmate. And now, as I look back on our journey together, I realize that our love has grown even stronger with each passing day.

"We may be separated by distance and time,

But our love knows no bounds,

And our hearts beat as one."

Through the trials and tribulations of life, our love has remained steadfast and true. I know that no matter where we are or what challenges we may face, our love will endure.

So, my beloved Reshma, I make this promise to you - to love you, to cherish you, and to hold you close, even across time and space.

Forever yours,

Badal

Also by Rajesh Giri

Scamming in the Shoe Market: An Inside Look
Still In Love With Her: A Guide To Sustain in a Long-Term Relationship
Beyond Time and Space: A Love That Endures
Love at First Write: Balancing Love and Creativity

About the Author

Rajesh Kumar Giri is a renowned lecturer of Mathematics, content writer, and a Practical Success Coach. With a passion for writing academic and educational content, Rajesh guides and trains people worldwide, breaking the barriers of language and region with his simple and easy-to-understand writing skills.

Rajesh's journey began in a poor family in a remote area of West Champaran, where he faced numerous challenges in paying for higher education. Despite the obstacles, he persevered and completed his degree, taking his first steps towards educating people and sharing his rags-to-riches ideas. Today, he resides in New Delhi, the capital of India, with his beautiful wife and two lovely sons, and he remains dedicated to serving poor students by providing free education online and offline.

Rajesh has been writing content in the education, affiliate marketing, and health niches since 2006. He believes that experiences speak louder than imaginary and bookish ideas, and his words connect with readers and result in conversions. As a Practical Success Coach, he helps people overcome their limiting beliefs and achieve their goals through practical techniques and strategies.

With his wealth of experience and passion for writing, Rajesh is committed to helping people around the world unlock their full potential and achieve success in all areas of their lives.